Dear Parents and Educators,

Welcome to Penguin Young Readers! As parents and educators, you know that each child develops at his or her own pace—in terms of speech, critical thinking, and, of course, reading. Penguin Young Readers recognizes this fact. As a result, each Penguin Young Readers book is assigned a traditional easy-to-read level (1–4) as well as a Guided Reading Level (A–P). Both of these systems will help you choose the right book for your child. Please refer to the back of each book for specific leveling information. Penguin Young Readers features esteemed authors and illustrators, stories about favorite characters, fascinating nonfiction, and more!

Dick and Jane: We Play

LEVEL **1**

GUIDED READING LEVEL **D**

This book is perfect for an **Emergent Reader** who:
- can read in a left-to-right and top-to-bottom progression;
- can recognize some beginning and ending letter sounds;
- can use picture clues to help tell the story; and
- can understand the basic plot and sequence of simple stories.

Here are some **activities** you can do during and after reading this book:
- Humor helps to engage children when they are reading. In this book, a lot of the humor is shown through the art. For example, on page 27, it says, "Oh, funny, funny Father." When you look at the picture, you can see what is so funny—Father's shoe has come off! Look at the pictures in the book, and discuss the ways in which they are funny.
- Sight Words: Sight words are frequently used words that readers must know just by looking at them. These words are known instantly, on sight. Knowing these words helps children develop into efficient readers. As you read the story, point out the sight words below.

can	funny	look	run	up
come	go	red	see	you

Remember, sharing the love of reading with a child is the best gift you can give!

—Bonnie Bader, EdM
   Penguin Young Readers program

*Penguin Young Readers are leveled by independent reviewers applying the standards developed by Irene Fountas and Gay Su Pinnell in *Matching Books to Readers: Using Leveled Books in Guided Reading*, Heinemann, 1999.

PENGUIN YOUNG READERS
Published by the Penguin Group
Penguin Group (USA) LLC
375 Hudson Street
New York, New York 10014, USA

USA | Canada | UK | Ireland | Australia | New Zealand | India | South Africa | China

penguin.com
A Penguin Random House Company

Dick and Jane is a registered trademark of Addison-Wesley Educational Publishers, Inc. From THE NEW WE WORK AND PLAY. Copyright © 1956 by Scott, Foresman and Company, copyright renewed 1984. From WE READ PICTURES. Copyright © 1951 by Scott, Foresman and Company, copyright renewed 1979. From WE READ MORE PICTURES. Copyright © 1951 by Scott, Foresman and Company, copyright renewed 1979. From THE NEW BEFORE WE READ. Copyright © 1956 by Scott, Foresman and Company, copyright renewed 1984. From THE NEW WE COME AND GO. Copyright © 1956 by Scott, Foresman and Company, copyright renewed 1984. All rights reserved. First published in 2004 by Grosset & Dunlap, an imprint of Penguin Group (USA) Inc. Published in 2012 by Penguin Young Readers, an imprint of Penguin Group (USA) Inc., 345 Hudson Street, New York, New York 10014. Manufactured in China.

Library of Congress Control Number: 2003016831

ISBN 978-0-448-43410-0   20 19 18 17 16 15

Dick and Jane
We Play

Penguin Young Readers
An Imprint of Penguin Group (USA) Inc.

Contents

Chapter 1
Play

Oh, Father.

See funny Dick.

Dick can play.

Oh, Mother.

Oh, Father.

Jane can play.

Sally can play.

9

Oh, Father.

See Spot.

Funny, funny Spot.

Spot can play.

Chapter 2
See Dick Play

Look, Jane.

Look, look.

Look and see.

See Father play.

See Dick play.

Look, Mother.

Look, Mother, look.

See Father.

See Father and Dick.

Oh, Mother.

See Spot.

Look, Mother, look.

Spot can help Dick.

Chapter 3
Funny Spot

Come, Spot.

Come, come.

Play, Spot.

Play, play.

Go, Spot.

Go, go.

Spot can play.

Dick can play.

Oh, oh.

Funny, funny Spot.

Chapter 4

See Spot Play

See Jane jump.

Jump, jump.

See Spot jump.

Jump, jump.

Oh, Dick.

Oh, Jane.

See Spot.

Funny, funny Spot.

Spot can play.

Chapter 5
Funny Father

"Come, Jane," said Father.

"Come and play ball.

Come and play."

"I can help you play ball,"

said Father.

"I can help."

"Come, Father," said Jane.

"Come and play ball.

Come and play."

Oh, funny, funny Father.

Chapter 6
Play Ball

"Come, Jane," said Father.

"Come and play ball.

Come and play."

"Oh," said Jane.

"See the red ball go.

See it go up, up, up.

Run, Dick, run."

"Oh, oh," said Dick.

"Where is my ball?

I can not find it.

Come here, Jane.

Run and help me.

Help me find my red ball."

"I can help you," said Jane.

"We can find the red ball."

Dick said, "I see it.

I see my red ball.

Look, Father.

See where it is.

Come and help me."

Jane said, "Oh, Dick.

Spot can help you.

Spot can find the ball."